Goldilocks
AND THE
Three Bears

A Parragon Book

Published by
Parragon Books,
Unit 13-17, Avonbridge Trading Estate,
Atlantic Road, Avonmouth, Bristol BS11 9QD

Produced by
The Templar Company plc,
Pippbrook Mill, London Road, Dorking, Surrey RH4 1JE

Designed by Mark Kingsley-Monks

Printed and bound in Italy

ISBN 0-75250-758-3

Goldilocks
— AND THE —
Three Bears

Retold by Caroline Repchuck
Illustrated by Nigel McMullen

Once upon a time there lived three bears; a big, gruff father bear; a kind, sweet mother bear; and a little wee baby bear.

The Three Bears lived all together in a cosy little house right in the middle of a great, green forest.

Father Bear was a good carpenter and had filled the little house with lots of lovely furniture. His favourite thing was a fine carved table that sat in the middle of the bears' kitchen.

Every day the Three Bears sat round the table to eat their breakfast, and their lunch and their tea. Then when they had finished, they sat in their

three chairs by the fire. There was a big chair for Father Bear, a middle-sized chair for Mother Bear and a little, small, wee chair for Baby Bear.

Upstairs, Father Bear had made three beds and a wardrobe for their bear necessities.

There was a great big bed for Father Bear, a soft, squashy middle-sized bed for Mother Bear and a little, small, wee bed for Baby Bear.

The Three Bears loved their home and thought the forest was a wonderful place to live.

Every morning they sat down to a delicious breakfast of porridge.

"It builds you big and strong!" boomed Father Bear, as he sat down.

"It warms up your tummy!" smiled Mother Bear, as she served up three steaming bowlfuls, sprinkled with sugar.

"And it tastes yummy!" giggled Baby Bear, covering his in honey.

There was a large porridge bowl for Father Bear, a middle-sized porridge bowl for Mother Bear, and a little, small, wee porridge bowl for Baby Bear.

Now, one sunny morning the Three Bears all sat down together to have their breakfast but their porridge was much too hot to eat.

"Let's go for a walk in the forest while our breakfast cools down," said Father Bear.

While they were out a little girl with long golden hair came walking by. Her name was Goldilocks.

"What a sweet house," she said. "I wonder if anyone is home?"

Goldilocks peeked through the window and saw the porridge on the table. "Mmm, that looks good," she said, licking her lips.

And, as no one was home, Goldilocks opened the door and went inside.

Now Goldilocks was a naughty little girl, and did not wait to be invited to breakfast. She just sat down and helped herself!

First she tasted Father Bear's porridge, but that was too hot. Then she tasted Mother Bear's porridge, but that was too cold. So then she tried Baby Bear's porridge. It wasn't too hot and it wasn't too cold. It was just right! Soon she had eaten Baby Bear's porridge all up!

Goldilocks felt full after her big breakfast, and wanted to sit down.

First she tried Father Bear's chair, but it was too hard. Then she tried Mother Bear's, but it was too soft. Then she tried Baby Bear's little chair. It wasn't too hard and it wasn't too soft. It was just right. But as she sat back, with a creak and a crash, the little chair snapped under her weight!

Goldilocks went upstairs to see if she could find a nice bed to lie on instead. First she tried Father Bear's bed, but it was too high to climb into. Then she tried Mother Bear's bed, but it was too soft and too low.

Then she spotted Baby Bear's bed. It wasn't too high, and it wasn't too low. It was just right!

So Goldilocks climbed in and was soon fast asleep.

Soon the Three Bears arrived
home from their walk. Straightaway
they knew something was wrong.

"Someone's been eating my
porridge!" roared Father Bear.

"And someone's been eating *my*
porridge!" growled Mother Bear.

Then little, small, wee Baby Bear looked at his empty bowl.

"Someone's been eating my porridge," he squeaked, "and they've eaten it all up!"

The Three Bears looked carefully around the room, in case their visitor was hiding there somewhere. They soon noticed that everything looked out of place.

"Someone's been sitting in my chair," bellowed Father Bear.

"And someone's been sitting in *my* chair," grunted Mother Bear.

Baby Bear looked around for his little, wee chair, but all that was left of it was a pile of wood in the middle of the carpet!

"Someone's been sitting in my chair," he wailed, and they've broken it into pieces!"

The Three Bears decided to hunt the house until they found their naughty visitor. Upstairs they saw at once that their beds were crumpled.

"Someone's been sleeping in my bed!" grumbled Father Bear.

"And someone's been sleeping in *my* bed," rumbled Mother Bear.

Baby Bear looked at his bed, and there, tucked up fast asleep, was a little girl with golden hair!

"Someone's been sleeping in my bed," he squealed, "and she's still there!"

Baby Bear's high squeaky voice woke Goldilocks at once, and she had a dreadful fright when she saw the Three Bears looking down at her!

She jumped out of bed and ran down the stairs as fast as her legs could carry her! She didn't stop running until she was far away from the little house, and the Three Bears never saw Goldilocks again!

The origin of this story is uncertain but the first printed version of *The Three Bears* appeared in 1837 and was written by the poet, Robert Southey. His story, however, is almost certainly based on a traditional folk tale where instead of Goldilocks, an angry old woman enters the house and samples the porridge!
Over the years the old woman changed into a little girl called Silver-Hair, then Silverlocks and finally ended up as Goldilocks in a new version of the story printed in 1904. The rest of the story has remained exactly the same but nobody has ever seemed quite certain how to give it a satisfactory ending. Some early versions had the old woman taken to a House of Correction by the village constable; one had her thrown "aloft on St Paul's church-yard steeple", but most end with Goldilocks simply running off into the wood, never to be seen again!